EGMONT
We bring stories to life

This edition published in Great Britain 2010 by Dean,
an imprint of Egmont UK Limited
239 Kensington High Street, London W8 6SA
All Rights Reserved

HiT entertainment

ISBN 978 0 6035 6412 3
5 7 9 10 8 6 4
Printed in Malaysia

Henry and
the Flagpole

All the engines on the Island of
Sodor were very excited. There
was soon to be a banquet at the
Scottish Castle. Thomas was being
a Really Useful Engine, he had to
make sure everything was ready on
time. There would be food, games
and bagpipe playing and The Fat
Controller would wear his kilt!

Meanwhile, Henry was also working very hard. He was steaming across Sodor, pulling trucks full of supplies for the banquet.

As he puffed through the forest, he spotted his favourite tree. Seeing the Tall Pine Tree made Henry very happy.

As he arrived at the Scottish Castle, Henry noticed that The Fat Controller was waiting for him.

"The castle's flagpole is too old,"
The Fat Controller explained.
"It could fall down and hurt
someone at the party. Henry,
I need you to collect the new
flagpole from the Docks in time
for the banquet."

"Yes sir," puffed Henry. He knew
this was a very important job.

Henry chugged into the Docks.
He couldn't see the flagpole
anywhere! He looked high and
low but could not find it.

Then Henry saw Cranky. He was
so busy saying "Hello," to him that
he puffed straight into a flatbed
truck with the flagpole on it.
"Whoops!" Henry cried, as the
flagpole rolled off the flatbed
and onto the next track.

"You weren't looking where you were going," snapped Cranky. Henry felt very silly. Just then, there was a loud CRASH. Salty had run over the flagpole!

"The flagpole's broken!" the Dock Manager cried.

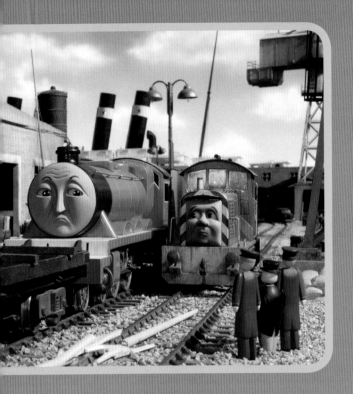

Soon, The Fat Controller
arrived, he looked very cross.
"This is a disaster," he boomed.
"The Scottish Castle will not look
the same without its flagpole."
Henry was very sad, it was all
his fault.

That evening, Henry was puffing
back through the forest.

"Maybe seeing the Tall Pine Tree will
cheer me up," Henry huffed.

But not even the Tall Pine Tree
could make Henry feel better.
Toby pulled up beside him and saw
that Henry was sad.

"I wish I hadn't broken the flagpole,"
Henry sighed.

"Maybe they could make a new
flagpole out of one of these tall
trees," Toby puffed, trying to cheer
Henry up.

Henry was very worried, he really
didn't want the Tall Pine Tree to be
cut down.

The next morning, Henry pulled
out of Tidmouth Sheds. He had
to take some workmen to the
forest. He could see they were
carrying axes and saws.

"Oh, no," wheeshed Henry.
"They must be going to cut down
my Tall Pine Tree."

Henry was worried. "Must save
the tree! Must save the tree!" he
chuffed to himself as he made his
way towards the forest. Suddenly,
Henry had an idea! He wouldn't
take the workmen to the forest,
he would look for a new flagpole!

The workmen noticed he was
going the wrong way. "This isn't
the way to the forest," said one
of the workmen.

But Henry wasn't listening.
He was looking for a new flagpole.

Henry puffed past the beach.
There was a large red and green
flag flying there. The flagpole was
tall, but not tall enough. "Bother,"
wheeshed Henry, sadly. "I'll never
save the Tall Pine Tree."

That evening, The Fat Controller came to see Henry at the Sheds. "Henry, those workmen had a very important job to do, you have caused a delay," he said, sternly. "Tomorrow, you will take coal to the Docks."

The next day, Henry puffed
sadly through the countryside.
"Soon they'll cut down the
Tall Pine Tree," huffed Henry.
"And I'll never see it again."

Henry was collecting the coal
when Thomas arrived. He explained
what had happened.

"I can't find another flagpole,"
said Henry. "I've looked everywhere!"

"I'd look again," puffed Thomas.
"Sometimes, I find things in places
I'd never thought of!"

Later that day, Henry was puffing across the countryside. "Where can I look that I wouldn't think of looking?" he wondered.

Henry looked around. He couldn't
see anything that would make a
good flagpole. He puffed past the
Orchard, but he only saw Trevor.

"Trevor is very nice," puffed Henry.
"But he wouldn't make a very
good flagpole."

Henry puffed sadly into the Docks.
"I've looked everywhere," he sighed.
"And I still couldn't find a flagpole."
Suddenly, Henry's face brightened.
"What about the old ship's mast?!"
he puffed.
"It's going to be used for firewood,"
Salty said.
"But it will be perfect for the
Castle flagpole," Henry chuffed.

Henry was excited. At last, he had found a new flagpole and where he'd least expected it, too.

Cranky lowered the ship's mast on to a flatbed truck, and Henry raced across the countryside, pulling it towards the forest. He had to get to the Tall Pine Tree, before they cut it down.

When Henry arrived at the forest, the Tall Pine Tree was still there. He showed The Fat Controller the ship's mast and he was delighted. "So, you won't cut the Tall Pine Tree down?" asked Henry.

"I would never cut the Tall Pine Tree down," exclaimed The Fat Controller. "The workmen are here to collect firewood for a roaring fire at the Scottish Castle Banquet."

Henry was so happy his axles tingled!

That evening, when Henry arrived at the Scottish Castle, the workmen were waiting at the station, ready to put up the new flagpole.

The flag was soon hoisted up and
it moved gently in the breeze.
It was the nicest thing Henry had
seen, except for the Tall Pine Tree!